Walking Lightly

Walking Lightly

a story by Fleur Beale

illustrated by Michaela Sangl

SIMPLY READ BOOKS

For Jane

Published in 2006 by Simply Read Books
www.simplyreadbooks.com

First published by Mallinson Rendel Publishers Ltd.

Text ©2006 Fleur Beale
Illustrations ©2006 Michaela Sangl

ISBN-10 1-894965-37-X
ISBN-13 978-1894-96537-8

CIP data available from Library and Archives Canada and
The Library of Congress

10 9 8 7 6 5 4 3 2 1

Design by Hamish Thompson and Michaela Sangl
Typeset by Hamish Thompson
Printed and bound in Canada

Contents

1.
Meeting Millie

Once upon a time, not very long ago and not very far away, there lived a girl called Millie. Millie's parents were rich. They had pots of money. They had cauldrons of the stuff, vats of it, tanks of it.

That's a heap of money. You'd think they'd buy
Millie everything a girl could dream of having,
plus a bit extra just for fun.

Quite a bit of everything a girl could dream of:

TV

DVD Player

mini trampoline

play stations

face goo

hair goo

body goo

bubbly soap

pet poodle

spa bath

make-up

cordless phone

pet cat with long hair to brush

cell phone

computer

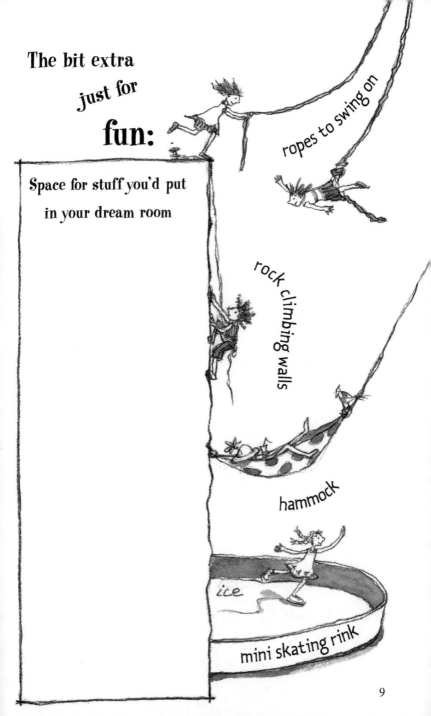

The bit extra

just for

fun:

ropes to swing on

Space for stuff you'd put
in your dream room

rock climbing walls

hammock

ice

mini skating rink

9

But that wasn't what happened because Millie was
a girl of extreme independence.

'I don't need all that stuff, thanks all the same,'
she said.

'Fair enough,' said Dad, 'but why not?'

'I want to walk lightly through the world,'
said Millie.

'Fair enough,' said Mom, 'but you had better
be prepared.'

'You need to be a girl of extreme resource as well
as a girl of extreme independence,' said Dad.

'Fair enough,' said Millie.

And so it was that when the other kids at her school took their holidays in:

Disneyland

ritzy ski resorts

exclusive tropical resorts with curved swimming pools

theme parks with water slides,

scary rides, boring rides

outer space

Millie spent her holidays camping, tramping, fishing, mountaineering, all the time learning how to take care of herself in a strange environment. She took with her only her strong boots and what she could carry on her back.

At school, the other kids said, 'You're weird!'
Henry didn't say it out loud, but he did think it.
Millie glared at them, including Henry.
They shuffled their feet and cleared their throats.
Millie was definitely weird, but she was fierce as
well. To calm her down, they showed her the stuff
they'd brought back from their holidays.

The latest

computer games

designer clothes

designer shoes

designer electronics

designer pets

music

hair goo

face goo

body goo

CDs

DVDs.

What Millie thought was: All that stuff! Did they buy a bigger car-plane-ship-train to carry it all? But she was so pleased they were being friendly and actually talking to her, that what she said out loud was, 'Amazing! Lots of stuff!' Then she fished in her bag and pulled out what she'd brought back from her holiday in New Zealand.

One packet of photos of:

a tui[1]

waterfalls

a kereru[2] feasting on karaka[3] berries

a **dead** boar
(her father killed it)

a mountain she'd climbed to the **top** of

the place where they had to wait for the river to go down before they could cross it

the hut where they stayed with 27 other wet, **smelly** people

the delicious fungi they ate when they ran out of food.

---

[1] *The tui is a bird of the honey-eating family found in the forests of New Zealand.*
[2] *The kereru is a native New Zealand wood pigeon.*

What the other kids said:

A tui! So what? They're boring.

So what? I've seen Niagara.

That's just a pigeon. I saw a cassowary[4].

It's a dead pig! Disgusting!

I went up the Eiffel Tower.

Use the bridge! Dumb! (and weird!) (Millie didn't bother pointing out that there was no bridge.)

Ultra-disgusting! Mega dumb!

No way!

You should only eat stuff you buy in a store!

---

[3] *The berries of the New Zealand karaka tree ripen from green to bright orange and provide food for the kereru.*

[4] *The cassowary is a large bird found in Australia and New Guinea.*

The kids looked at her, turned up their noses and pulled down their mouths. So Millie didn't show them the scratches on her legs, the scar on her hand or the perfect skeleton of a leaf she had found.

They walked away, shaking their heads and muttering under their breaths. Henry walked away too, but he only shook his head. Definitely, she was weird. He shrugged his shoulders, took out his new game and switched it on. Then he switched it off and marched back to Millie.

She was putting her photos back in her bag.

'Hmmm,' he thought, staring hard. 'She doesn't look weird right now — or fierce. She looks sad.'

He sat down beside her.

Now she looked surprised.

He felt sorry for her,

always sitting on her own,

always walking   by herself.

'Why don't you like new stuff?' he asked. 'And stuff like bridges that can help you cross flooded rivers?'

A surprised sort of smile snuck around Millie's mouth. Somebody was talking to her! It was all very well being a person of extreme resource and independence, but she did get lonely.

Henry grinned back at her, and she jumped. Somebody was smiling at her! Her own half-grown smile stretched out into a grin.

'So?' he asked again. 'Why don't you ever have new stuff? Exciting stuff?'

'But I do!' Millie said.

'I got a new pack last year. And the best boots for Christmas. I get stuff whenever I need it. You should see my camera.'

Henry stared at her, shook his head and shrugged his shoulders. Millie's grin shrank and died. She watched him wander away and she sighed a huge sigh that came right up from where her boots would be if she'd been wearing them.

Friends. She'd like friends. You could have loads, piles, heaps, mountains and oceans of friends and still walk lightly through the world. But she didn't have even a sniff of a friend. It was a pity money couldn't buy friends. She'd be into the Friend Shop quicker than a rock could skedaddle down a mountain.

'Can I have two friends, please?'

'Certainly, miss. What sort?'

'The friendly sort. The sort who won't care that I'm a person of extreme resource and independence. Or that I'm weird.'

She sighed again and thought hard about mountains, lakes and oceans to cheer herself up.

2.
Millie's Experiment

That night, Mom and Dad said as usual, 'How was school?'

Usually Millie said, 'Fine.' Then she'd say, 'What'll we do this weekend?' But tonight she said, 'Fine. I guess.'

Her parents, being people of unusual sensitivity, knew immediately what the trouble was.

Mom said, 'Millie, you'll have to try harder to make friends.'

Dad passed her the dessert. 'Do the things they like. It won't hurt you. You might even enjoy it.'

Millie put a big helping of rhubarb and strawberry pie on her plate. 'All right,' she said. She took a deep breath. 'How about we go shopping this weekend?'

'Okay,' said Dad. 'That's a good start. What do you need? Are your boots pinching? Flashlight batteries flat? A hole in your socks?'

'Everything's fine,' said Millie. 'I don't *need* anything.'

Mom and Dad stared at her — gobsmacked. There's no other word for it. Unless the word is hornswoggled. Gobsmacked and hornswoggled.

'Er,' said Dad. 'Shopping?'

'Shopping as in buying *frivolous* things?' demanded Mom.

Millie nodded her head in a determined sort of way. 'They all like shopping. They shop every week. Every day. All the time. We'll go shopping.'

So they went to the mall.

Hetty and Awa from school saw her and giggled. 'Look! Would you believe it! There's Weird Millie! In the mall. With her *parents*!'

Lucky for Millie, she didn't see them. She was too busy being confused by all the stuff.

There were:
racks of clothes
stacks of shoes
jungles of electronics
oceans of lotions

'I can't do this!' Millie wailed.

'You don't have to buy it all,' said Dad.

Mom looked around. She started walking. 'Come on. Clothes shop. Buy jeans. Buy a top.'

Millie tried on a pair of jeans. She bought them. She tried on a top. She bought it. 'Now what?'

They all looked at each other and shrugged. 'Let's go to the mountains,' they said.

On Monday, Millie wore her new clothes to school. The kids took one look and giggled. 'Millie's so *weird*!' they said, and they didn't whisper either.

Then they forgot about her and showed each other the things they'd bought.

shiny necklaces   big watches   rings

tiny phones   DVDs   shoes   bikes

CDs

tiny games   tiny computers   skateboards

They saw Millie watching them. She had a frown on her face, but it was from puzzlement — she just didn't get it. But Jacquie said, 'Ooh! Fierce Millie is frowning at us! She's so *weird*!'

Henry glared at them and smiled at Millie.

Millie tried to smile back, but it turned into a sigh. It was each to her own. 'We'll never meet in the middle,' she thought.

She sat by herself in class. She ate by herself at lunchtime. She walked home by herself after school. 'I'd have fun shopping at a Friend Shop,' she thought.

Ingredients Millie decided she'd ask for in a friend:

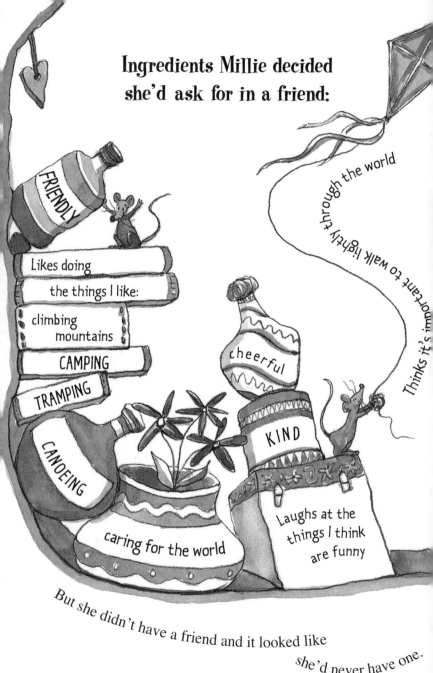

FRIENDLY

Likes doing

the things I like:

climbing mountains

CAMPING

TRAMPING

CANOEING

cheerful

KIND

caring for the world

Laughs at the things I think are funny

Thinks it's important to walk lightly through the world

But she didn't have a friend and it looked like she'd never have one.

Your list of friend ingredients:

write in here

write here

write here too!

Things went on like that for a month or two, then a year or two. The other kids kept on going on swanky holidays, watching TV, playing computer games and lying around chatting to each other on their phones.

'Millie's weird,' they said to each other. But they didn't say it to her any more because Millie got more and more fierce the more they laughed at her or ignored her.

3.
The Brilliant Idea

One day somebody at the school had a brilliant idea. 'Let's show our children how other people live.'

Everyone said, 'My goodness! What a brilliant idea!'

The teachers and parents talked about it.

Fabulous idea! Let's go and see how people live in very cold places.

But we went to **The Alps Grand Ski Resort** for the holidays. We know how people live in very cold places.

Okay, then let's go and see how

people live in

tropical places.

But we went ...

We could go again.

Okay, let's organise it.
Let's go to a

tropical

island.

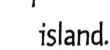

The kids and the teachers and the parents made lists like this:

1 Air-conditioned bus to travel in
2 Air-conditioned hotel to stay in
3 Maps
4 Global Positioning Device
5 Cell phones
6 Computer games (for when they got bored.)
7 Face goo, hair goo, body goo
8 Clothes (they could only take three suitcases each, no bigger than 90 cm x 45 cm and that caused a lot of howling and moaning.)
9 Strong shoes for walking ('Walking shoes! We're not going to walk,' everyone said.)
10 Cameras (digital, video, polaroid)

Millie went home and told her parents about the trip to a tropical island to see how other people live. 'They're crazy,' she said. 'I'm not going.'

'Hmm,' said Dad, 'perhaps you'd better go. They'll need someone with extraordinary resource and independence.'

'If you don't go,' said Mom, 'who will rescue them when they get into trouble?'

Millie sighed. 'Fair enough. But I'm warning you — it'll be a bit of a mission.'

'You can cope,' they said. And Millie knew she could, but to be on the safe side, she researched the tropical island:

on the internet

at the library (books, encyclopedias, magazines)

by talking to people who had been there

The other kids did research too. They went to travel agents and got shiny brochures with glossy pictures of:

deluxe resorts

people with smiling faces

nifty launches to go on guided fishing trips

Three weeks later all the kids said they were ready to go. They all said proudly,

They had:

designer swim suits • designer sun hats • designer mosquito nets
designer shorts, shirts (two changes of everything for each day)
sandals (no walking shoes) • face goo • hair goo
body goo • phones • hair dryers • hand held video games

'I've managed to get my gear into just three suitcases and one carry bag.'

hand held battery operated fans • spare batteries

cameras: video, digital and polaroid • underwear for each day

plus three spares • sleep wear (one set for each night because it was

hot in the tropics even though the hotel was air conditioned)

Millie wore her strong boots and took only what she could carry on her back. In her pack she put:

three changes of shorts • T-shirts • underwear • one sweatshirt

an extra T-shirt to sleep in • sun hat • swim suit

mosquito net • sun screen • Swiss army knife • matches

strong rope • mug • plate • flashlight

Stuff you'd take to a tropical island:

She carried her camera and four books on to
the plane with her.
The kids whispered, 'Millie's weird all right.'

4.
Getting There

Everyone got on the plane and flew for as many hours as it took to get there.

What the kids moaned about on the plane:

I want to be in **first** class.

There's not enough room for my knees.

The movie's b o r i n g .

The food's d i s GUSTING!

The seats are

uncomfortable.

I don't want to sit next to:

Millie
Henry
Kyle
Hetty
a stranger
Awa
Mr or Mrs Candy
Ms Bunn
Felix
a baby
a smelly person
ANYONE!

Millie rolled her eyes, opened her book, read and smiled at the air crew whenever they gave her anything.

The trip ended.

Everyone got on to the air-conditioned bus and went to the air-conditioned hotel.

'Cool!' they said. They jumped in warm showers and used all the face goo, hair goo and body goo the hotel had put there. Then they jumped in the curved swimming pool and washed it all off.

Millie sat under a tree and finished her book.

The next day everyone got back on the air-conditioned bus. 'We're going into the hills to see how other people live,' said the teachers.

Things the kids said as they drove along:

My game's **boring**. Let's swap.

My phone **won't work**.

I don't want to get **mud** on my sandals.

I'm **not** swimming in a river.

There'd better be hamburgers for lunch. I'm **starving**.

Does my shirt look **good** with this skirt?

Millie rolled her eyes and rested her feet on her pack.

Things the kids said as they drove along:

kids with big bush knives

working in gardens

kids in uniform working in a school room

a river falling over rocks

women washing laundry in the river

boys playing soccer

a woman carrying a load of

banana leaves on her head

a man chopping fire wood with a big bush knife

The road got **narrow**

and bumpy

and **STEEP**

The kids moaned:

I **HATE** this!

This is a **dumb** place to live.

whine moan grizzle

5.
The Catastrophe

The catastrophe happened just before lunch. It wasn't the sort of catastrophe Millie had been expecting. It was bigger and she just knew it was going to be way more difficult than anything she had dreamed of.

The first inkling that something unusual was happening came when the bus gave an extra big bounce.

Some kids screamed, some cheered and Kyle threw up the twelve chocolate bars he'd eaten into his hat.

Mrs. Candy screeched, 'This road's a disgrace!'

Mr. Candy bellowed, 'An utter, complete and total disgrace!'

'We'll sue!' they shouted together. Millie suspected they practised.

The bus jolted and jerked down the last bit of a very steep hill. The road they were on wasn't a smooth highway, but it wasn't bad enough to make the bus buck and bounce.

Then a boulder bounced past Millie's window.

She screamed.

Just a tiny scream.

Eeek!

Boulders, she knew, had no business to be bouncing down a road. Buses sometimes had reason to bounce, but not boulders.

A bouncing boulder was not a good thing.

She knelt
on her seat.
She had plenty
of room because,
as usual, she sat by
herself. She looked back at
the road they'd travelled down.

It wasn't there.

She frowned.

Above the noise of the
engine and the shrieking
of the kids and the Candys,
she heard a medley of noises
followed by a large

45

BUMP

The jolt FLUNG Millie around in her seat

Or were supposed to be going

But they weren't moving, Millie realized.

All around her, the earth heaVed

and BILLOWED

so she was looking again in the direction they were going.

Not forwards, anyway.

and BuC**K**ED

as if it had turned into a **stormy sea.**

'Oh, no,' she groaned, 'an earthquake!' She held on tight to her seat and tight to her tongue. No way was she going to yell and scream and screech like the Candys, Francie, Kyle and Sherry were doing. Although she wanted to.

Henry's voice reached her through the din. 'You okay, Millie?'

'Ecstatically wonderful!' she shouted back.

She heard him laugh and a little grin of her own crept out.

The swinging and the swaying slowed. The jolting and the jerking faded and died — with just the odd hiccup to remind everybody that this was no ordinary day.

'An earthquake!' screeched Mr. and Mrs. Candy. 'We're definitely going to sue the socks off somebody!'

Millie heard a mutter. It came from Henry. 'God, perhaps?'

She giggled.

'Earthquake! Earthquake!'
     the driver screamed.
     He opened the door,
jumped out
     and ran away

into the jungle,

which was difficult to do since most of it lay every which way on top of itself.

Millie knelt on her seat again and looked back. The road behind had shaken itself right off the side of the very steep hill. She looked forward. The road in front had turned into a pile of rocks, cracks and lumps.

She slumped down into her seat.

'Oh no!' she said. 'We won't be going anywhere very fast for a very long time.'

She looked around the bus. Everyone was screeching and wailing, gasping and groaning.

Get us **out** of here!

CALL:

the police

an ambulance

the army

a helicopter

They all dived for their cell phones. None of them worked. Millie knew they wouldn't. She'd checked it out before she left home. She rather wished she was still at home.

The teachers and the parent helpers (except the Candys) clapped their hands. 'Come now! Be calm. We'll have lunch.'

'We should ration it,' Millie said. 'It's the only food we've got and it's going to have to last for days till we get rescued.'

'Nonsense!' said the parent helpers, and they frowned at her. 'They'll have us out of here in no time.'

'We've got the Global Positioning Device,' said the teachers. 'The rescuers will know exactly where to find us.' They gave Millie the kind of look that said: Don't say another word if you know what's good for you.

Millie sighed again, but she knew it was useless arguing. She ate her lunch (bread rolls filled with lettuce, tomato, egg, chicken, cheese and cucumber). But she saved her three chocolate bars and the apple for her dinner.

By dinner time everyone else was moaning and groaning, screeching and wailing.

I'm hungry!

Starving!

Famished!

Why haven't they rescued us yet?

We'll sue them.

I wanna go home NOW!

Millie took her knife out of her pack
and quietly set about making herself a
shelter of banana leaves and a bed of
ferns. No way was she going to sleep
in the bus with the moans and groans,
the screeching and the wailing.

When she had finished, she went into
the bush to see what she could find.
She came back with papayas, bananas,
coconuts and sugar cane.

'Oh yuck!' said the kids (except for Henry who ate three bananas and a papaya). 'The bananas have got marks on them. Coconuts don't look like that in the supermarket. I don't believe you — no way is that sugar cane.' They prodded the papayas. 'We're not eating *those*!'

'Fair enough,' said Millie. She crawled into her shelter, pulled the mosquito net over her and had an extremely good night's sleep.

6.
Finding out how other people live

In the morning everyone fell on the bananas and papayas. 'Yum! Get us more!' they yelled.

Millie said, 'Come with me and I'll show you how to get it yourselves.'

Four of the girls, five of the boys and Mr. and Mrs. Candy said, 'No, I'd rather starve than:

go into the jungle

get my sandals dirty

do any work

let a kid boss me around.'

'Fair enough,' said Millie, 'but I'm thinking you'll get hungry.'

She was right. By lunchtime they ran after
her. They scrambled over the fallen trees, the
uprooted palms and didn't care that branches
ripped at their clothes.

They tore whole bunches of bananas off the palms and shoved them into their mouths — skin and all. It wasn't a pretty sight.

That night, as everyone but Millie climbed back in the bus to try and sleep, they said, 'We'll definitely be rescued tomorrow.'

'Don't bet any money on it,' Millie muttered. She noticed Henry looking around at the broken hills, the mashed trees. He had a thoughtful look on his face.

In the morning Millie built a fish trap in the river. (Luckily the river was still flowing out to sea.) While she was making it she asked the kids,

the teachers and the parent helpers to gather
wood for a fire.

Ooh! There might be spiders!
Scorpions!
Snakes!
Ooh! That's work!
No kid tells me what to do.
No way! I came here to see how other people live,
not to work.

Then Henry said, 'You want to eat — you have to
work. This is how other people live.'

So they all worked, and that day they ate:

fish baked in clay
yams cooked in the ashes
papayas
bananas
pineapple

and it was good.

7.
What the papers said back home

Back home,
this is what the newspapers said:

Our son could be **dead,** cry distraught parents.

We'll sue! outraged parents threaten.

Why can't they find them? demand anguished friends.

Millie's mom and dad read the papers. 'Hmm,' said Dad, 'maybe we'd better do something.' 'Nobody else is,' said Mom, 'so I guess it's up to us.'

They hired a fast ship, put a helicopter on the deck, and sailed off to the tropical island. They got there just in time to share the pig Millie was roasting.

'A PIG!'

cried her parents.

'My goodness, how did you manage that?'

Millie grinned. 'A rock fell on its head and killed it. Henry found it.'

All the kids, the teachers and the parent helpers crowded around Millie's parents.

We've had an **awesome** time.
Look! I washed my own clothes! In the river!
We **know how to**:

cook fish • find food in the bush • build a shelter to sleep in.

We know how **other** people live.

Mom and Dad hugged Millie.
'Well done,' they said.

What the kids and some of the adults said about Millie:

We'd have starved to death without Millie.

She saved our lives.

She's remarkably resourceful. For a child.

Millie knows things.

Millie showed us what to do.

She's actually a really nice person. When you get to know her.

Millie's cool.

Millie grinned a huge grin. 'Thanks,' she said. 'Let's have some roast pork.'

After lunch they all tidied up and the helicopter flew them back to the fast ship. But before they sailed home, they helped fix up houses the earthquake had damaged. When they left three weeks later, they each gave their three suitcases of gear to people who had lost stuff when their houses fell down.

Millie's parents presented the helicopter to the island people. Millie donated her pack, her boots, her camera and her books, even though she was worried about having nothing to read on the way home. She sighed. It was going to take days to get home, even though it was a fast ship, days of being bored and lonely.

But, as it turned out, she had no time to read, no time to be bored and she absolutely wasn't lonely. All the kids talked to her. They made her join in when they sang or played keep-out-of-the-way-

of-the-sailors-in-case-they-give-us-work-to-do.
(Some of the kids hadn't changed that much.)
They asked her questions. They started lots of
conversations with, 'Hey, Millie, remember when
you showed us how to . . .'

Why you would rather travel by
ship, or why you'd much rather
travel by plane, particularly
if the Candys were on board.

When they got home, everybody showed the reporters and photographers their scratched arms and legs. 'Now we know a little bit about how other people live,' they said.

'And we're going to raise money to help the people on the island. All their gardens and orchards are wrecked.' That was Hetty's idea and she nagged at everyone and made them work together. 'Even you,' she said to Millie.

So for weeks they all worked together. They organised:

fairs

baby shows

concerts

guess how many diamonds in a jar competition

garage sales where they sold all the gear they didn't use any more

'I've run out of ideas,' said Hetty. 'It's your turn, Millie. You're a person of extreme resource and independence. You think of something.'

So Millie did. She thought of a fun run and a guided mountain walk.

Most of the kids and some of the adults did it. Twenty-three percent of them enjoyed it.

Henry loved the run and the walk. Hetty adored the run (she won) and she thought she could get used to walking in the mountains.

Awa hated the run but loved the walk.

Not one person said Millie was weird — but, of course, Mr. and Mrs. Candy weren't there.

After a month, the teachers counted up the money.

'Well done,' said the teachers. 'That's a lot of money. It'll help the people. We must get the TV cameras along when we send it off.'

So they did. The Candys were there for that.

Millie, Henry, Hetty and Awa smiled to themselves.

8.
How Millie found out about how other people live

The next Friday, Hetty and Awa sat down beside Millie. 'What are you doing this weekend?' they asked.

'Nothing special,' said Millie. Mom and Dad had said they needed to catch their breaths after taking part in all the fund-raising.

'That's good,' said Hetty, 'because you're going to come shopping with us. We're going to show you how to survive in our world.'

A grin stretched itself across Millie's face. 'Fair enough,' she said.

So they went to the mall. Millie learned that she didn't have to buy the first thing she saw.

She learned that some things looked good on her and some things looked as if she was going to some weird party where you had to dress as badly as you possibly could.

She learned that when you're with friends you can have a lot of fun even if what you're doing isn't really your thing.

What Millie bought at the mall:

one top that looked good on her

one skirt that looked good on her

books to send to the people on the island

a roll of film for the camera she'd bought when she got back from the island

The next weekend she said to Henry, Awa and Hetty, 'Would you like to come canoeing?'

So they did.

And it was good